Michael Broad lives in Surrey on Planet Earth, where he writes and illustrates books for children of all ages, including the Jake Cake series, which was shortlisted for the Waterstone's Prize. Michael loves dogs, daydreaming and anything to do with astronomy.

www.michaelbroad.co.uk

*Other books by Michael Broad*

Spacemutts: Attack of the Ninja Kittens!

# MICHAEL BROAD

SPACE MUTTS

Fluffy Assassins from Mars!

MACMILLAN CHILDREN'S BOOKS

First published 2011 by Macmillan Children's Books
a division of Macmillan Publishers Limited
20 New Wharf Road, London N1 9RR
Basingstoke and Oxford
Associated companies throughout the world
www.panmacmillan.com

ISBN 978-0-330-51140-7

3 5 7 9 8 6 4 2

A CIP catalogue record for this book is available from
the British Library.

Printed and bound by CPI Group (UK) Ltd, Croydon, CR0 4YY

*For Harvey*

*(a super shih-tzu mix)*

# The Alien Invasion

Have you ever looked up at the stars and wondered if aliens really exist? Well, they do! Lots of them! All across the galaxy bright green eyes are looking right back at us, studying our world as they prepare to invade it.

Some aliens already walk among us, but they don't have slimy skin or wiggly tentacles. They're cute and fluffy, eat fish and chase mice, and if they're not already living in your home, you've probably seen them in your garden.

That's right – all cats are aliens from outer space! Tiddles from next door is in charge of weapons. Pickle from the post office relays intergalactic orders. And the big ginger tom who lets you tickle his belly on your way to school is an expert in explosives.

It's true that some cats are harmless and happy just being our pets, but if you watch the others closely you'll see they're up to something. Most of them are spies, plotting in secret and preparing for the invasion. Cats have ruled the rest of the galaxy for thousands of years, conquering every habitable world, and now their sights are set on Earth to complete their evil empire.

The feline forces have tried to invade

our planet many times before, which is how so many cats got stranded here. But they were always doomed to fail because Earth is home to the best alien defence force in the universe . . .

# THE SPACEMUTTS

*When night falls on the Pooch Pound*

*dogs' home, these courageous canines*

*board their spaceship and patrol the*

*galaxy.* Man's best friend defending

*the Earth against cosmic kitty cats.*

# THE DOGS

**ROCKET** Fearless leader
of the Spacemutts

**POPPY** Plucky pilot of the
spaceship *Dogstar*

**BUTCH** Inventor, dribbler
and all-round genius

**SCAMP** New recruit
(an eager beagle)

# THE CATS

**LADY FLUFFKINS** Evil empress of the entire galaxy (well, almost)

**BALDY** Cowardly minion of Lady Fluffkins

**THE FELINE FORCES** Every breed of cat across the galaxy!

# Contents

# The Pooch Pound

'WOOF! WOOF! WOOF!'

Rocket barked at the top of his voice, which meant a family were visiting the Pooch Pound looking for a dog to re-home. As the family walked down the row of kennels the big brown mutt made as much noise as possible, and this set off the other dogs in the next two kennels.

Poppy chased her tail in rapid circles, yapping like a mad thing, while Butch howled and growled, and dribbled all over the floor. The only dog behaving himself was a beagle puppy called Scamp, who offered his paw, wagged his tail, and rolled over for a belly rub. He'd only

arrived at the kennels that morning, but didn't plan on staying very long.

Scamp gave a whimper as the family were led away and hoped they could hear it over the racket coming from the other kennels. The three other dogs upped their bad behaviour as the humans passed by, but when the warden closed the door the room fell silent.

'It's a bit late for visitors,' said Butch, lifting a paw and wiping the drool from his mouth.

'I thought they'd never leave!' panted

Poppy. 'Tail-chasing is tiring work!'

Both dogs looked at Rocket, who was standing at the bars with his head tilted. 'It's OK, they're locking up now,' he said, ears twitching at distant sounds. 'And the night warden has just arrived.'

What did he have for dinner?

Butch asked eagerly.

Rocket lifted his shiny black nose and sniffed the air.

Sausage and mash,

he said.

'Ooooh, sausages,' sighed Butch, and started drooling again.

'That's a pretty big dinner for a night shift,' said Poppy. 'I'll give him five minutes before he's sleeping like a baby.'

Rocket and Butch nodded in agreement and all three settled down on their blankets to wait. Their routine was the same every evening, and the dogs knew they could do nothing until the warden was asleep.

'Do you think they liked me?' said a small voice from the far kennel.

The three dogs frowned and turned

to look at Scamp, who was peering at them through the mesh. Rocket, Poppy and Butch had lived together for so long that they often forgot about the fourth kennel.

'The family that just left,' said Scamp. 'Do you think they liked me?'

Oh, I'm sure they did,

said Poppy.

You were very well behaved and really cute.

I licked their faces and everything!

chuckled the beagle pup.

'Smart dog,' said Butch. 'You'll be out of here in no time.'

'That's the plan,' said Scamp, scratching his neck with a rear paw. 'But why do you three act so badly when the humans come? You must know it puts them off taking you home.'

'We have our reasons,' said Rocket, wandering back over to the bars.

The dog lowered his head and listened carefully for the familiar sound of snoring, and after a few minutes he nodded to Poppy and Butch, who quickly leapt up.

Scamp watched in amazement as the three dogs sprang into action, dragging their blankets into dog-shaped heaps and clearing away water bowls and chew toys.

Then they bounded to the centre of their kennels and sat beneath the domed lights.

What's going on?

asked Scamp.

'You should move into the corner of your kennel,' whispered Poppy.

'Can't we bring the pup with us?' suggested Butch.

'He's much too young,' said Poppy. 'And he's had no training.'

'I'm house-trained!' the beagle stated proudly.

Poppy and Butch looked at Rocket.

'The pup should stay behind,' he said.

Scamp had no idea what was going on, but knew whatever it was he was being left out. The little dog slouched into the corner, circled his blanket a few times, and flopped down with a heavy sigh.

In the centre of his kennel, Rocket swiped his collar with a paw and the chrome spikes lit up around his neck.

> This is Rocket calling the *Dogstar* . . . Come in, *Dogstar*.

'Good evening, Captain,' said a female voice, each word making the collar-lights blink. 'I'm orbiting Earth directly above your location, all systems are fine and the teleport is prepped for boarding.'

'Then beam us up,' said Rocket. 'Over and out.'

Scamp jumped up and tilted his head as the glowing domes above each kennel buzzed and flickered on and off. Then four shafts of light shot down from the ceiling. The beagle watched with wide eyes as the three dogs sparkled and shimmered, and then disappeared one by one. Butch was the first to go, quickly followed by Poppy. Rocket remained a moment longer and then looked back at the eager beagle.

Scamp gave a hopeful 'YAP!'

'Oh, come on then,' smiled Rocket.

Scamp wagged his tail frantically and scrabbled on the spot, bunching up the blanket with his hind legs. Then he leaped from the corner straight into the beam. The two dogs sparkled briefly before the room went dark, and when the dome lights flickered on again, the kennels were all empty.

Far across the galaxy, in the Catnip Nebula, Lady Fluffkins gazed at the spiral of stars from the bridge of her clockwork *Mouseship*. This was the white Persian's favourite place to view her galactic empire. From here she could see the entire Milky Way.

'Look at its swirly-whirly creaminess,' she said, licking her whiskers.

'Yes, My Lady,' said Baldy, fiddling nervously with his tail. The hairless servant searched his mind for a compliment, because the empress insisted on a constant stream of flattery.

'It is a magnificent sight, and proof of your, um . . .'

'Proof of my what?' she spat. 'Quickly, you bald buffoon!'

'Genius!' gasped the quivering cat. 'Proof of your *genius*!'

'Then why does one puny planet continue to elude me?' demanded Lady Fluffkins, fiddling with the controls on the intergalactic telescope. She tapped in a familiar set of coordinates and waited.

'Because of the dogs, mistress . . .' said Baldy.

'Oh, yes,' hissed the empress, green eyes flaring with fury. 'Because of fleabag

Rocket and his meddling Spacemutts. The dumb doggy defence against my fabulous feline empire.'

The pair watched the monitor as the telescope scanned the cosmos, closing in on a small solar system and narrowing its focus on the third planet from the sun. When Earth appeared on the screen Lady Fluffkins arched her back, hissed, and then swiped at it with her paws as if trying to claw at a ball of wool.

Baldy watched from a safe distance until the empress exhausted herself and flopped back in her throne. Then he pulled out a fan and wafted it over her long white fur, knowing how sudden fits of rage overheated his mistress.

'Well, those mangy mutts can't protect it forever,' gasped Fluffkins, prodding the telescope with a hind paw and shifting its view to the fourth planet in the solar system. 'How are things progressing on the red planet?'

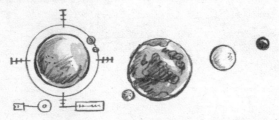

'All ready to go, gracious one,' said Baldy. 'Just waiting for your wondrously wicked word.'

'Excellent,' purred the empress,

drumming her long, sharp claws on the armrests.

> Send orders ahead that we invade Earth tonight, and then prep the *Mouseship* for a wormhole jump to Mars!

# The Spotty Planet

On the deck of the *Dogstar*, four teleport beams whooshed up from the floor and four doggy shapes sparkled in the light. When the beams dropped away, Rocket, Poppy and Butch immediately leaped to their stations, leaving a wide-eyed Scamp to watch in wonder.

The spaceship was like a big chrome

tank with bolted panels and round portholes, and its curved walls were covered with wires, switches and small flashing lights.

Rocket jumped up to the central hub, where he began rolling out star maps and scanning screens. The hub controlled all the deep-space telescopes and spy-bone satellites monitoring the galaxy.

Poppy took her usual seat in the cockpit and switched from autopilot to manual controls, while Butch went to the back of the ship and sniffed around the mechanics.

# SPACEMUTTS

'Anything to report, WOOF?' said Rocket, without looking up.

'Nothing unusual, Captain,' said the female voice Scamp had heard earlier, but it wasn't coming from Rocket's collar – it seemed to come from the ship itself. 'And I see you've brought along a new recruit.'

'I'm Scamp,' said the pup, looking around for the owner of the voice.

'WOOF is the ship's computer,' said

Poppy, glancing back from her station. 'It stands for World Orbiting Observation Facility. She circles the planet during the day, making sure no one enters Earth's orbit while we're on the ground.'

Scamp joined Poppy at the front of the ship and gazed into space through the main observation window. The young pup often looked up at the stars when he lived on the streets, but he had never seen them shining so brightly.

'Impressive, huh?' said Poppy.

Scamp was too amazed to speak, so he nodded eagerly.

Then he trotted over to Butch, who was
sniffing around under a silver sheet that
covered something large and long at the
back of the ship. Scamp tried to sneak
a peek, but Butch gave a low warning

growl. Butch was always inventing something, but would never let anyone see it until it was completed.

The young dog got the message and quickly moved over to Rocket, who had just finished scanning all the intergalactic data and was satisfied that planet Earth was in no immediate danger. He saw Scamp peering up at him and lifted the pup on to the podium.

'I expect you have a lot of questions, little one,' said Rocket.

'Er, not really,' said Scamp.

'Huh?' said Rocket, who was never

usually lost for words.

'You're the Spacemutts!' said Scamp. 'You travel the galaxy in the *Dogstar* making sure Earth doesn't get invaded by evil empress Lady Fluffkins and her cosmic cats!'

Er, yes,

said Rocket.

But how . . . ?

'Oh, you're *really* famous on the streets,' said Scamp. 'The alley dogs talk about you all the time. One even said he'd been on adventures with you, but I thought he was making it up.'

'What was his name?' asked Butch.

'Bonkers,' said Scamp. 'He was a retired greyhound.'

'Ah, good old Bonkers,' said Butch. 'He lets the dog-catchers bring him in from time to time, and comes along with us for the ride. There's not a cat in the whole galaxy that can outrun Bonkers!'

'So you know all about us,' said Rocket.

Yes, Captain, and I'm ready for my first intergalactic adventure!

'No adventures tonight,' said Rocket, patting the pup's head. 'I've been through all the data and everything is as it should be out there. No feline fleets or humongous hairballs hurtling our way.'

'There must be something going on with all those planets filled with mean old cats!' said Scamp. He pulled down the periscope and peered through it with a determined growl. 'I bet I can find *something*!'

'I'm afraid you won't find *anything* through that,' laughed Rocket. 'The

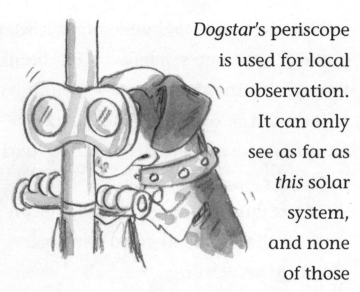

*Dogstar*'s periscope is used for local observation. It can only see as far as *this* solar system, and none of those planets are inhabited.'

'Not even the spotty one?' said Scamp.

'What spotty one?' Rocket frowned. 'There isn't a spotty planet in our solar system.'

'The red one with white spots,' said Scamp, adjusting the focus. 'And I think it's getting spottier . . .'

Rocket quickly moved his paw over the touch screen on the hub and transferred the periscope's signal to the giant monitor. Butch hurried over to join them and Poppy swung round in her chair.

'That's Mars!' gasped the Spacemutts as the red planet appeared on the screen.

They all leaned closer and frowned at the rash of white spots that had mysteriously appeared on the planet's surface. More spots were popping up as the dogs watched the live feed from the periscope.

'Well, I've never heard of a planet getting pimples,' growled Rocket. 'WOOF, can you confirm that nothing has entered our solar system in the past twenty-four hours?'

'That's affirmative, Captain,' said WOOF.

'Then keep a close eye on Mars for any

unusual activity,' said Rocket, rolling out a map of the solar system and calculating the distance from Earth. 'Butch, fire up the light-speed engines!'

'Already on it, Captain!' said Butch, hurrying away.

Rocket then bounded over to the pilot station as Poppy swung back to her controls. He leaped up beside her and stared into space. 'Set a course for Mars, Poppy,' he said. 'Something very strange is happening on that red planet, and I don't think it's chickenpox.'

'Right away, Captain,' said Poppy, flicking switches on the control panel.

Butch raced up and

down at the back
of the ship, pulling down levers and
adjusting pressure valves. Under his
expert paws the *Dogstar* engines rattled

and hissed into life, then Butch called out to the pilot.

Light-speed in five, four, three, two, one!

he barked.

On the count of one, Poppy pushed all acceleration levers forward and the *Dogstar* soared through space so fast that the stars shifted in the inky sky. Scamp

jumped from the podium and ran to the
front of the ship where he peered over
the controls. The pup could see the red
planet glowing in the distance, growing
bigger as they shot towards it
at the speed of light.

**3**

# A Smashing Invention

The *Dogstar* hurtled towards Mars like a silver comet, but before it broke through the atmosphere, Poppy quickly pulled back on the levers and Butch stabilized the engines. With the ship orbiting the red planet, Rocket returned to the periscope and swung it towards the surface.

The dogs quickly gathered round the

central hub as the monitor showed a close-up image of the giant white circles that were scattered across the Martian landscape.

'Flying saucers!' the Spacemutts gasped together.

'But how did they get here without us seeing them?' said Poppy, knowing nothing could get this close to Earth without WOOF picking up a signal. 'We pass by this planet all the time – they can't have just appeared from nowhere!'

Rocket adjusted the periscope's focus and zoomed in on one of the flying saucers. All four dogs gave a low growl when they saw the small fluffy creatures

sweeping the shiny white craft with their bushy tails. The cats were as rusty orange as Martian rocks.

'Ginger tabbies!' barked Butch.

'But how did they get here?' asked Poppy.

'I think there's a very good chance they've always been here,' said Rocket. 'Their fur is the exact same colour as the surface of the planet, which makes them practically invisible. Those crafty cats must have been building a

secret squadron for years, keeping them buried below the surface.'

'A complicated craft like that would rust and scratch under Martian soil, not to mention dust getting in the engine,' said Butch. 'They must have built them with some other material.'

'However they did it they're preparing to make their move,' said Poppy, as the last of the flying saucers was swept clean. 'Which means Lady Fluffkins must be nearby. The empress can't resist giving a speech before an invasion.'

'How do we stop so many saucers?'

asked Scamp, who was feeling a bit left out and wanted to get in on the action.

'What did you say?' Rocket frowned.

'How do we stop them?' repeated Scamp. 'I'm a Spacemutt too, and I want to help . . .'

'No, you called them *saucers*!' said Rocket, scratching his chin.

'What are you thinking, Captain?' asked Poppy.

'Well, we know from past experience that Lady Fluffkins likes her invasions to have a kitty-cat theme,' he said, zooming in on one of the shiny white crafts.

'Maybe she's finally lost her marbles and confused *flying* saucers with the type of saucer you fill with milk . . .'

'You don't mean . . . ?' said Poppy, wondering if it was even possible.

'The saucers are made of china!' exclaimed Butch, piecing it all together. 'A china craft would not only be light

and airtight, but it can be buried underground for years without coming to any harm. It's pretty clever when you think about it.'

'Or really, really stupid.' Rocket smiled. 'Because china has one other quality that could work in our favour.'

'It's very easy to SMASH!' said Scamp, quickly catching on.

'But there are so many of them!' said Poppy, who had counted over a hundred of the craft. 'How can we possibly bring a whole fleet down with one little ship?'

'Well, I have been working on

something,' said Butch, biting his lip.

Rocket raised an interested brow.

'But it's nowhere near finished,' Butch added quickly. 'And it's probably much too risky to even attempt. On second thoughts, forget I even mentioned it. It's definitely too dangerous.'

The Spacemutts all looked at Butch, who dribbled on the floor.

Then he trotted to the back of the ship and pulled the silver sheet from his mysterious invention. To Scamp and the other two frowning Spacemutts it was just a mess of wires and circuits with a

large funnel at the top and a long barrel sticking out at the front.

'What's that?' they all said together.

'The Cat Litter Cannon!' said Butch, pointing to various parts of the

contraption. 'You fill the funnel with litter, here, and fire it through the cannon, here. And when the cats see all that lovely litter they'll forget their evil plans and want to have a wee instead!'

And you think that will work?

Poppy frowned.

Of course not, it's a terrible idea,

said Butch moving over to a diagram on the wall and scribbling a quick equation. 'But if I narrow the cannon and increase the firing pressure, one grain of litter should be enough shatter a giant china saucer.'

Brilliant! said Rocket.

But what's so dangerous about that?

'There's no time to wire it into the *Dogstar*'s mainframe,' said Butch. 'So we'll have to strap it to the front of the ship, where one of us will need to operate it manually. And it will have to be someone small enough to fit behind the cannon.'

Rocket, Poppy and Butch all looked at the beagle pup.

'I'll do it!' said Scamp, wagging his tail excitedly.

Just then the warning lights began

to throb across the control panels and a siren sounded through the ship. 'WORMHOLE OPENING OVER PLANET MARS!' said WOOF, in a louder, more serious voice than usual. 'MOUSESHIP SIGNATURE DETECTED!'

'Get us down to the surface, Poppy,' said Rocket, knowing their plan would fail if Fluffkins saw the *Dogstar* circling Mars. He scanned the Martian landscape

and quickly located a large enough crater to land in, where they could also prepare the cannon without being seen.

Poppy bounded back to her seat as Rocket sent her the coordinates and Butch prepared the ship for a rapid descent. As the *Dogstar* fired its engines and shot down through the orange atmosphere, Scamp looked back in time to see a spiral vortex ripping through the starry sky.

# Flight of the
# Flying Saucers

The wormhole opened above the red
planet in a swirling tunnel of purple
light, and through it came the clockwork *Mouseship*, key turning and tail
spinning as it zipped through space and
time.

The metal mouse burst through the

atmosphere of Mars with a clap of thunder and began hurtling towards the ground. At the last minute, two wheels appeared from its underbelly and the *Mouseship* bumped along the red, rocky surface, rattling to a stop before the vast saucer squadron.

## Fluffy Assassins from Mars!

A metal door dropped down with a clang and Baldy scuttled out with a pile of satin cushions, placing them in a line from the base of the *Mouseship* to a tall podium with a giant screen behind it. Moments later, Lady Fluffkins stepped from the ship and made her slinky way

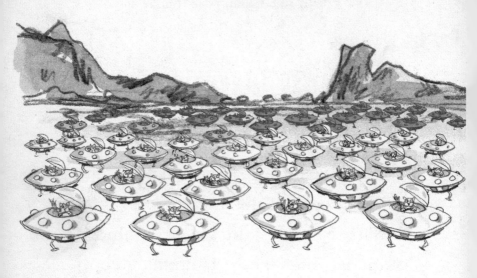

along the row of cushions, head and tail held high.

The tabby troops meowed from their saucers as the white Persian stepped up to the podium and appeared on the screen, and fell silent when she tapped the microphone. Lady Fluffkins then

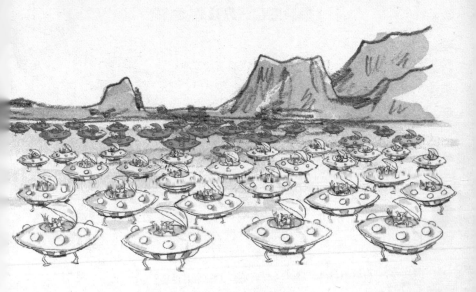

leaned forward, cleared a large hairball from her throat and spat it out in front of her.

'Earth!' she purred, spinning the matted ball playfully with her paw. 'A small blue planet filled with mangy mutts and dumb, hairless creatures that

call themselves humans.'

Baldy glanced down at his pink, fleshy body and gulped.

'But the time of man and man's best friend has come to an end,' the empress continued. 'Martian moggies! You have built this magnificent fleet right under the dogs' stupid wet noses, and tonight you will invade planet Earth and complete my glorious empire!'

A yowling cheer erupted from the feline fleet, followed by the humming of

engines as the flying saucers all hovered above the ground. Lady Fluffkins kept them waiting a moment longer as she squashed the hairball beneath her paw, then the Persian slowly lifted her head.

'FLY, MY GINGER PRETTIES! FLY!' she roared, and swiped the squashed hairball from the podium. With that the fleet of flying saucers took to the sky, leaving a cloud of dust in their wake.

When the dust settled, Lady Fluffkins frowned at the sound of rumbling jets coming from a nearby crater. She looked at Baldy, who shrugged helplessly. Then

the empress gave a deafening YOWL! as the *Dogstar* slowly rose up above the podium and took off after the saucers.

The *Dogstar* gave chase to the flying saucers with the modified Cat Litter Cannon strapped to its nose. Poppy had to crane her neck sideways in the pilot seat to see where she was going, while Rocket watched nervously as Scamp made practice swings with the weapon. The pup wore a harness around his belly to hold him steady and goggles to protect his eyes from dusty Martian winds.

'The engines are now at maximum power!' Butch barked from the back of the ship.

Poppy pushed the levers forward and

quickly closed in on the feline fleet. The plan was simple: shatter the soaring saucers and then return to Mars to capture Lady Fluffkins.

The Spacemutts all watched nervously as Scamp focussed his sights on the fleeing craft, and held their breath

as the first round of litter streamed from the cannon. The shower of grit shot through the sky at bullet speed, but missed the flying saucers completely.

'Give him time,' said Poppy, pulling the *Dogstar* around for another attempt.

'He's just warming up,' said Butch, adjusting the fuel valves.

Rocket nodded and held his breath, though at that moment the captain was more worried about the safety of the pup than the threat of the enemy craft.

When the *Dogstar* came about, Scamp knew to pull the cannon to the right on firing, and this time the torrent of litter showered through the saucers, immediately shattering half of the fleet. China pieces filled the sky like exploding

fireworks, with ginger tabbies shooting through the air in ejector seats.

The beagle waved a triumphant paw and the Spacemutts cheered his success. Then Poppy zoomed around the falling debris and took off after the remaining saucers. With expert steering, she managed to gather most of the saucers together like a sheepdog herding sheep, and Scamp shattered them in a rapid fly-past. Then they took off after the few remaining craft, who looped the loop and spun wildly, but were no match for the nimble *Dogstar*.

The beagle pup was now more confident, swinging the cannon back and forth, and firing short bursts of litter as the china craft fled in all directions. CRACK! SMASH! CRASH! they went, and the sky was filled with a blizzard of broken crockery.

With Butch keeping power levels up and Poppy steering under Rocket's

orders, Scamp made short work of the remaining feline flect. Working as one, the Spacemutts quickly cleared the sky of saucers, smashing all except one, which had doubled back and was flying close to the ground.

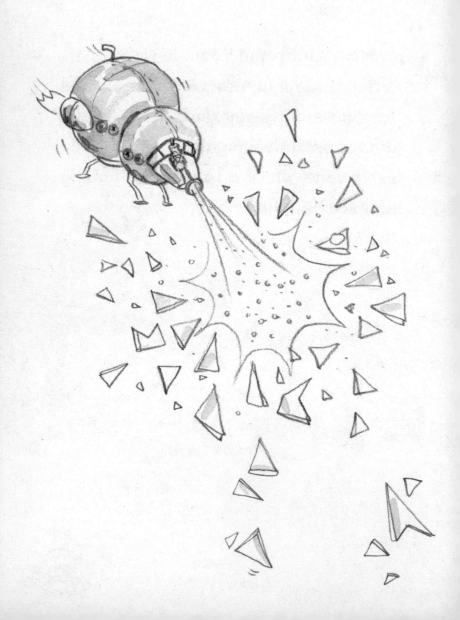

## Fluffy Assassins from Mars!

'After him, Poppy!' said Rocket.

The *Dogstar* took a vertical dive and then gave chase mere metres above the ground. Scamp swung the cannon wildly to get a shot, but the saucer kept pulling back alongside their ship, just out of range.

Rocket and Poppy growled as the ginger minion poked his tongue out at the beagle pup, shamelessly taunting him.

Scamp tried desperately to swing the cannon round for a sideways shot, but the safety harness holding him to the ship made that impossible. So the pup unfastened the buckle and clung to the weapon as it spun round the nose of the *Dogstar*. Scamp quickly dispatched the saucer with one short burst, but the cannon kicked back and knocked the pup clear from the ship.

'NOOOOO!' yelled Rocket, watching the pup fall. The captain immediately bounded to the back of the *Dogstar* and threw open the cargo doors. He gulped at the red, rocky ground speeding past below him and then leaped from the rear of the ship.

Rocket hit the ground hard and rolled in the dust to lessen the impact, then he sprang up and looked around for Scamp. The pup was still tumbling along the dusty surface of the planet, and eventually bumped to a stop at the base of Lady Fluffkins' stage.

Rocket bolted forward as fast as he could, but the white Persian had been watching everything. The empress moved like lightning to the edge of the platform and then leaped on the helpless pup.

# Bye-bye, Beagle

Rocket skidded to a halt as Lady Fluffkins landed on the dazed pup, pinning him down with all four paws. The captain lowered his head and gave a rumbling growl, circling the Persian and her puppy prisoner.

'One step closer, Spacemutt,' hissed Lady Fluffkins, 'and it's bye-bye, beagle!'

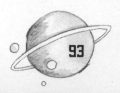

'Let him go, furball!' growled Rocket.

'After he broke all of my lovely saucers?' hissed the cat. 'Not likely!'

'He was acting under my orders,' barked the captain as he continued to stalk around the Persian, slowly closing the circle. 'I'm the one you *really* want!'

'Hmmm,' purred the cat, with a twinkle in her eye. 'That's true!'

In one rapid movement Lady Fluffkins leaped from Scamp and on to Rocket's back, hackles high and tail puffed out like a pompom. She immediately dug

her claws in and began screeching like a wild thing as the dog bucked to throw her off.

'YEOOOOW!' shrieked Fluffkins, leaping on to the dog's head and tugging at his ears.

'GRRRRRR!' growled Rocket, rolling on to his back to shake her free.

Fluffkins and Rocket separated and stalked around each other like sparring scorpions, growling and hissing, before the surprisingly strong Persian pounced again and knocked the dog on to his back.

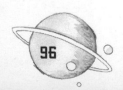

A few metres away Baldy crept out from under the podium and was just wondering whether to assist his mistress when Scamp sprang up and gave a low growl. The cowardly minion immediately thought better of it and shot back into his hiding place.

Lady Fluffkins and Rocket fought like cat and dog, rolling around in a cloud of red dust with paws swiping and fur flying. The cat

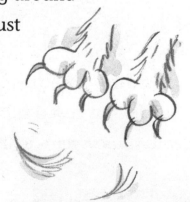

was smaller than the dog, but twice as fast and with sharper claws. However, when the dust finally settled, Rocket was standing over the hissing, spitting ball of

white fur. The dog was exhausted, but he managed to hold the villain down.

'Your war against Earth is over, Fluffkins!' Rocket panted. 'I'm taking you back to the *Dogstar*, where you will be held in a maximum-security cat basket.'

'You really think you can catch me so easily, you foolish fleabag?' sneered the empress, smiling wickedly. 'I believe your dumb doggy brain has forgotten someone.'

Rocket looked around and then frowned at a cowering, hairless servant who was peeping out from beneath the stage.

'Not him!' scoffed the Persian, and

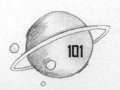

glanced up at the sky. 'Them!'

Rocket and Scamp were suddenly
aware that it was growing very dark,
as though a black cloud was passing
overhead. And when they looked up,

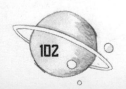

the sky was filled with hundreds of
parachuting ginger cats, all diving in
their direction.

 'Uh-oh!' said Rocket and Scamp
together.

Just then the pair spotted the *Dogstar* flying low, slipping in under the cloud of cats and skimming the ground ahead of them with its cargo doors still open. Rocket immediately grabbed Lady Fluffkins by the scruff of the neck and the two dogs bounded after the ship.

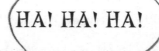

HA! HA! HA!

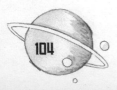

laughed the Persian, bouncing up and down below the dog's jaws.

Rocket growled through gritted teeth.

'I was just thinking that you can't possibly get me *and* the pup aboard that rust bucket,' she chuckled, as the first dozen tabbies thudded to the ground behind them. The cats cut their

parachutes loose and quickly gave chase. 'You'll notice he's already falling behind.'

Rocket glanced to the side and could see that Scamp was tiring, and the rapidly growing tide of tiny tigers was gaining on him. Fluffkins was right – he couldn't save the pup *and* apprehend her.

The *Dogstar* had slowed to close the distance between them, but it was still too far away to jump. Rocket was exhausted from the fight, but knew he had to find the energy for one final push.

The captain of the Spacemutts had

two choices. He could capture the evil empress and finally put an end to her evil war against planet Earth, or he could save one brave little puppy.

This decision was made in the blink of an eye.

Rocket immediately tossed Fluffkins over his head into the surging sea of ginger fur and snatched Scamp from the grasp of the ferocious felines, who had their claws out and were swiping at his tail. The dog then bounded with all his might towards the cargo hold, panting hard.

Poppy used all of her
piloting skills to keep the
*Dogstar* low and slow, and
Butch appeared at the back of
the ship, barking encouragement to his
captain.

The ginger cats were a whisker away
from pulling him down when Rocket
found a final burst of energy and threw

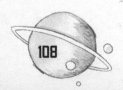

the pup to the safety of the ship, before jumping up after him. The *Dogstar* immediately closed its doors on the hissing cats and soared away.

As the *Dogstar* made its way back to Earth, Lady Fluffkins was stomping through a sea of ginger cats, angrily flicking red dust from her fur. The tabbies backed away as their empress made her way back to the

clockwork *Mouseship*. Before boarding, the Persian surveyed the ruined saucers scattered across the Martian landscape. The debris of broken china made Mars look like a winter wonderland.

'Clear this lot up!' she spat. 'I want this planet *spotless*!'

Then Fluffkins leaped inside her craft.

The terrified tabbies immediately spread out and began sweeping up the mess. It would take years to gather up every piece of china, and they knew this was their punishment for failure.

Baldy quickly gathered up the satin cushions and hurried after his mistress. The hairless servant immediately took the controls of the *Mouseship* and set a course back to the Catnip Nebula, while Lady Fluffkins sat seething in her throne. The empress said nothing for the entire journey home, and when they eventually

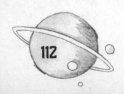

arrived Baldy waited nervously.

'I will get that little blue planet one day,' she hissed. 'And those mangy dogs

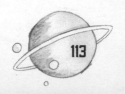

too!' she added, flicking out the claws on all four paws. 'But in the meantime . . .'

Baldy quickly crouched down because he knew what was coming.

'YAAOOOOWWW!' screeched Lady Fluffkins, leaping from her throne and landing on a giant scratch post at the centre of her ship. The Persian was a blur of white fur and claws as she attacked the tatty column, swiping and slashing and yowling with rage.

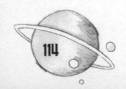

# The Solo Mission

Back on Earth, the dogs returned to their kennels in time for the morning rounds and before the first visitors of the day. Rocket, Poppy and Butch settled down on their blankets to rest, while Scamp paced up and down the bars. The beagle pup was tired too, but he had something on his mind.

'They'll be coming back again today,' said Poppy. 'And this time they'll take you home with them.'

'Who?' asked Scamp.

'The family that came to see you yesterday,' Poppy said, smiling.

'How do you know?' Scamp frowned.

'When you've been here as long as we have, you can tell,' said Poppy.

I gave them a good sniff, and they're decent people,

added Butch.

'They did seem very nice,' said Scamp. 'So maybe they'll take you three as well, if you behave yourselves when they come back. Then we could all live together!'

I'm afraid we still have a job to do,

said Rocket.

'Lady Fluffkins will be plotting another invasion, and the Spacemutts are Earth's only defence against the feline forces.'

'Then I'll stay too,' said Scamp. 'I'll nip the family's ankles when they come back. Then they won't want me any more and I can join the Spacemutts for good!'

'No,' Rocket said firmly. 'We need your eyes and ears out in the world, watching the Earth cats to make sure they're not planning an uprising of their own.'

'How?' asked the pup.

'If you see a cat in the garden, chase it

121

out!' said Rocket. 'Even if it's just perched on a wall – bark at it! Let them know we're always watching.'

'But you'll be a dog down if I leave!' said Scamp.

'Your kennel won't be empty for long and we will train up another new recruit,' said Rocket. 'But we will always remember the brave young pup who took down the Martian moggies.'

Poppy and Butch nodded in agreement.

'Proud to serve the Spacemutts!' said Scamp, and gave a paw salute.

A familiar scent filled Rocket's nose

and when the door suddenly opened, he started barking as loudly as he could. Poppy quickly jumped up and chased her tail in rapid circles, yapping like a mad thing. And Butch howled, growled and dribbled on the floor.

The family hurried past the three noisy dogs and crouched down when the warden opened Scamp's kennel. The little dog ran to them, wagging his tail and licking their happy faces. He couldn't wait to join his new family and was very keen to begin his solo mission.

As Scamp was led away the three dogs

winked, and the pup
gave a farewell 'YAP!' to
his friends.

When the warden
closed the door,
the kennels fell
silent again and
the three dogs
returned to their blankets to sleep, and to
dream about the day they would defeat
Lady Fluffkins once and for all. Then the
Spacemutts could stop growling and tail-
chasing and barking, and find happy
family homes of their own.

Maybe next time . . .

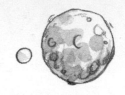

# SPACEMUTTS GALAXY GRAND SLAM GAMEPLAY

The more collector cards, the better the game!

To begin a new game, all cards are dealt face down between two or more players. The dealer then takes the topmost card from their pile and chooses a category to do BATTLE with the other player(s).

There are 6 categories, SIZE, BRAINS, SKILL, SPEED, CUNNING and STRENGTH, and each character has varying abilities. A small cat will obviously lose against a big dog in a BATTLE of SIZE, but could triumph in a BATTLE of CUNNING, so chose wisely.

The challenger reads out the number from their chosen category and the other player(s) reveal their score(s) from the same category. The player with the highest number wins the BATTLE, and all cards played in that round go to the bottom of their pile.

The winner of each BATTLE takes the next topmost card from their pile to begin a new round, and the ultimate GALAXY GRAND SLAM winner (and RULER OF THE ENTIRE GALAXY!) is the player left holding all of the cards.

# A selected list of titles available from Macmillan Children's Books

The prices shown below are correct at the time of going to press. However, Macmillan Publishers reserves the right to show new retail prices on covers, which may differ from those previously advertised.

---

## Michael Broad

| | | |
|---|---|---|
| Spacemutts: Attack of the Ninja Kittens! | 978-0-330-51141-4 | £4.99 |
| Spacemutts: Fluffy Assassins from Mars! | 978-0-330-51140-7 | £4.99 |
| Spacemutts: The Sausage Dog of Doom! | 978-0-330-51142-1 | £4.99 |

---

All Pan Macmillan titles can be ordered from our website, www.panmacmillan.com, or from your local bookshop and are also available by post from:

**Bookpost, PO Box 29, Douglas, Isle of Man IM99 1BQ**

Credit cards accepted. For details:
Telephone: 01624 677237
Fax: 01624 670923
Email: bookshop@enterprise.net
www.bookpost.co.uk

**Free postage and packing in the United Kingdom**